Amazing Snakes of the Northeast

Parker Holmes

PowerKiDS press.
New York

Published in 2015 by The Rosen Publishing Group, Inc.
29 East 21st Street, New York, NY 10010

First Edition

Editor: Jennifer Way
Book Design: Andrew Povolny
Photo Research: Katie Stryker

Photo Credits: Cover Steve McGuire/E+/Getty Images; p. 5 E R Degginger/Photo Researchers/Getty Images; pp. 6, 12 John Cancaliosi/Photo Library/Getty Images; pp. 7, 10 John Serrao/Photo Researchers/Getty Images; p. 9 James Gerholdt/Stockbyte/Getty Images; p. 13 Kenneth M Highfill/Photo Researchers/Getty Images; p. 15 Joe McDonald/Visuals Unlimited/Getty Images; pp. 16, 22 (bottom) Jason Patrick Ross/Shutterstock.com; p. 18 Scimat Scimat/Photo Resarchers/ Getty Images; pp. 19, 20 Paul Witten/Photo Researchers/Getty Images; p. 21 (top) Edward Kinsman/Photo Researchers/ Getty Images; p. 21 (bottom) Leonard Lee Rue III/Photo Researchers/Getty Images; p. 22 (top) Dennis Donohue/ Shutterstock.com; p. 22 (middle} Ryan M. Bolton/Shutterstock.com;

Library of Congress Cataloging-in-Publication Data

Holmes, Parker, author.
Amazing snakes of the Northeast / by Parker Holmes. — First edition.
pages cm. — (Amazing snakes)
Includes index.
ISBN 978-1-4777-6487-9 (library binding) — ISBN 978-1-4777-6488-6 (pbk.) —
ISBN 978-1-4777-6491-6 (6-pack)
1. Snakes—Northeastern States—Juvenile literature. I. Title.
QL666.O6H752 2015
597.96'0974—dc23

2013044854

Manufactured in the United States of America

CPSIA Compliance Information: Batch #WS14PK6: For Further Information contact Rosen Publishing, New York, New York at 1-800-237-9932

Contents

Seasonal Snakes

Snakes live all around us! They can be hiding in bushes, resting under rocks, or slithering in the grass. Snakes can be found throughout the country, and the Northeast has a variety of them. There are about 20 **species** of snakes in the Northeast. Most of them are harmless. Only two types of **venomous** snakes live here—rattlesnakes and copperheads. The copperhead is found only in the southern part of the region. Venomous snakes are what many people call poisonous snakes. You're much more likely to run into a harmless species, such as a garter, ringneck, racer, brown, or water snake.

Since the Northeast has cold winters, you won't see snakes here all the time. Snakes don't like chilly weather, so they **hibernate** and disappear for several months. But when the weather warms up, you just might run across one. Let's take a look at some exciting snakes of the Northeast.

The timber rattlesnake, shown here, is found in the northeastern United States in Vermont, New Hampshire, New York, New Jersey, Pennsylvania, Maryland, Connecticut, and Massachusetts.

Black Rat Snake

Black rat snakes are the biggest snakes in the Northeast. They often grow to around 5 feet (1.5 m) long, but they can get bigger. The record is 8.5 feet (2.6 m)! These **reptiles** are part of the rat snake group. You can probably guess their favorite food—rats and mice. Does that sound tasty to you? These snakes think they're yummy. They kill these rodents by wrapping their powerful coils around them and squeezing them to death. This squeezing is called **constriction**, so these kinds of snakes are called constrictors.

Black rat snakes are found throughout the Northeast, in parts of the South, and in parts of the Midwest. This one was photographed in New York.

Black rat snakes are dark colored, and people sometimes call them black snakes. They're good climbers, so you might find one in a tree looking for food, such as a bird or its eggs. If you see a black rat snake, don't worry. They're big and can look **intimidating**, but they're not venomous.

Here, a black rat snake is shown climbing up a tree trunk.

Eastern Garter Snake

If you spot a snake in your yard, it just might be a garter snake. There are lots of varieties of garter snakes. They're one of the most **abundant** snakes throughout the country. In the Northeast, the eastern garter snake is the most common variety. Some people call them garden snakes, but their real name is garter snakes. If you see one around the yard, don't be afraid. They're not dangerous. But if you pick them up, they may try to bite. They also might squirt you with stinky **musk** and poop. Yuck! Like most snakes, garter snakes prefer to be left alone.

Eastern garter snakes often grow to nearly 2 feet (61 cm), and they're usually dark colored with checkers and yellow stripes running down their backs. These snakes eat all kinds of small creatures, such as frogs, worms, lizards, and even fish.

The eastern garter snake is Massachusetts's state reptile.

Eastern Milk Snake

This eastern milk snake is guarding her eggs. A group of snake eggs is called a clutch.

You won't find too many eastern milk snakes crawling around in plain view. These secretive snakes often hide under logs and rocks during the day and come out at night to hunt. Milk snakes are part of the king snake group. They're constrictors, so they squeeze their food to death. They like to eat small mammals, such as mice, but will eat lots of different food, even other snakes. They typically reach 2 to 3 feet (61–91 cm) long. Eastern milk snakes are usually brown or gray with red or brown blotches. People sometimes confuse them with the similar-looking venomous copperhead.

Milk snakes seem to have gotten their name through a mistaken belief. These snakes sometimes hang out in barns, where they look for mice. So people thought the snakes might be sucking milk from the **udders** of the barn cows. That's definitely not true!

Timber Rattlesnake

This timber rattlesnake is eating a chipmunk.

If you see a venomous snake in the Northeast, it might be a timber rattlesnake. But don't get too close! You don't want to be bitten by one. These snakes have sharp fangs that inject venom. They use those fangs to hunt their favorite prey, such as mice and chipmunks. Timber rattlesnakes usually grow to 3 to 4 feet (91–122 cm). They often look brown with darker blotches.

Do you know why they're called timber rattlesnakes? "Timber" is another name for wood, and these snakes like to live in areas with thick forests. They also like rocky areas. The timber rattlesnake population has declined in some places, especially the New England states. If you do run across one, it might let you know by shaking its rattles—bzzzz! That's a warning to stay away! But these shy snakes aren't looking for a fight. They just want to be left alone.

Here, a timber rattlesnake is coiled and shaking its rattle. This is a warning to stay away!

Northern Black Racer

Black racers are fast! They're one of the fastest snakes in the country. That's why they're called racers. There are several types of racers, and the **subspecies** found in the Northeast is called a northern black racer. These snakes are built for speed. They're slender snakes that usually grow to between 3 and 5 feet (1–1.5 m). They're solid black, so some people call them black snakes. They're good climbers and will go into trees looking for a meal. Racers aren't picky eaters and like all kinds of critters, such as lizards, mice, and insects.

Racers aren't venomous, but they might bite if you mess with them. They're **feisty** snakes that don't usually like to be touched. As a warning to you, they'll even vibrate their tails against the ground, sounding sort of like a rattlesnake. That's their way of saying, "Please leave me alone!"

This northern black racer is hiding among the leaves.

Smooth Green Snake

The smooth green snake is small enough that it can slip nearly unnoticed through the grass.

Some snakes may look scary to you. But chances are, you're not going to be frightened by the smooth green snake. This little snake is bright green, nonvenomous, and almost never bites people.

You have to look hard just to find one. The smooth green snake is an expert at camouflage. That means it can blend in with the surroundings so that it's hard to see. Some people call green snakes grass snakes. This snake likes to hide in green grass and low bushes. This **disguise** helps it hunt for its favorite food—insects. The camouflage also protects the snake from **predators**. The green snake is small and skinny, usually about 12 to 18 inches (30–46 cm) long. So it's no match for a lot of animals that want to eat it, such as a hawk. The smooth green snake needs to be careful.

Northern Water Snake

Do you like to swim? So do northern water snakes. Whenever you see a snake near water in the Northeast, there's a good chance it's a northern water snake. They're very good swimmers. They like to live around swamps, ponds, lakes, and all kinds of watery places. These snakes don't spend all their time in the water. They spend a lot of time on shorelines or in branches overhanging water.

Here, a northern water snake is eating a fish whole.

This northern water snake is resting on a rock in the Delaware River in Pennsylvania.

Northern water snakes are usually brown with darker blotches. They're typically 2 to 3 feet (61–91 cm) but can be bigger. Water snakes aren't picky eaters. They eat all kinds of food, including lots of fish and frogs. Since they're not venomous snakes or constrictors, water snakes usually swallow their food while it's still alive. If you come across a water snake, it's best to leave it alone. Water snakes can be grouchy and often bite if you pick them up.

Variety Show

If you're searching for snakes in the Northeast, you might find a number of interesting types. Some of them are so small you have to look carefully just to find them. If you peek under rocks or inside rotting logs, you might uncover a tiny ringneck or red-bellied snake. These creatures are often less than 12 inches (46 cm) long. You have to look even harder to find the eastern worm snake.

Red-bellied snakes live throughout the Northeast. They eat insects, slugs, and earthworms.

Ringneck snakes, like this northern ringneck, are named for the bright ring around their necks.

This little snake spends much of its time underground looking for worms to eat. In your snake searches, you're more likely to come across a species such as a ribbon, brown, garter, or water snake.

Do snakes scare you? If they do, remember that most snakes in the Northeast are harmless. In fact, snakes do a lot of good. They help us by eating pesky insects and rodents. The Northeast has a lot of great snakes. Snakes here are fun to watch!

The northern brown snake is also known as the De Kay's snake.

Other Snakes in the Northeast

- Common ribbon snake
- Copperhead
- Eastern hognose snake
- Eastern kingsnake
- Eastern massasauga
- Eastern ribbon snake
- Kirtland's snake
- Mountain earth snake
- Northern scarlet snake
- Queen snake
- Rough green snake
- Short-headed garter snake
- Smooth earth snake

Copperhead

Eastern hognose snake

Queen snake

Glossary

abundant (uh-BUN-dent) More than enough, plentiful.

constriction (kun-STRIK-shun) The process by which some snakes kill their prey.

disguise (dis-GYZ) A change in the way one looks in order to hide one's identity, or what one is.

feisty (FY-stee) Quick to fight or show aggression.

hibernate (HY-bur-nayt) To spend the winter in a sleeplike state.

intimidating (in-TIH-muh-dayt-ing) Making shy or afraid.

musk (MUSK) Strong-smelling matter given off by an animal's body.

predators (PREH-duh-terz) Animals that kill other animals for food.

reptiles (REP-tylz) Cold-blooded animals with lungs and scales.

species (SPEE-sheez) A single kind of living thing. All people are one species.

subspecies (SUB-spee-sheez) Types within a species.

udders (UH-derz) Organs that hold milk in some animals.

venomous (VEH-nuh-mis) Having a poisonous bite.

Index

Websites

Due to the changing nature of Internet links, PowerKids Press has developed an online list of websites related to the subject of this book. This site is updated regularly. Please use this link to access the list:
www.powerkidslinks.com/amaz/neas/